BROKEN AND

BRUISED

A Short, Interesting, Enlightening Christian Story

Grateful West

APPRECIATION

My sincere gratitude goes to God for making this project become a success. I thank in for his inspiration. I thank him because this book will bless many lives.

I also appreciate my family and friends and also you, who is reading this book. Thank you.

CHAPTER ONE

Inspired by Holy Spirit.

It is a long weary day for beloved sister Deborah, work has really been hectic. As a young daughter of Zion, her deep alarm had begun to blow the trumpet reminding her of Bible Study and Quiet time. Suddenly, her phone starts ringing

"Who could be calling me at this dead hour of the day"? she blurted with worries and overwhelming tiredness as she dragged herself from the kitchen to pick her call.

Guess who the caller is? Bro Daniel

She rolled her eyes at the sight of the name, fuming seriously as she humbly and politely picked the call.

"Oh God what does this brother want again? I thought I finally told him I am not led to him" she groaned under her breathe.

'Sister Debby Debby! Why are you treating me this way? I have prayed seriously and I am assured I am led to you.

Just to think of it, yester night as I was praying, I asked God for another confirmation and boom a brother came to my apartment and everything he was just talking about is the distinct Deborah in the Bible.

I love you and I can't deny this, please don't let this love be a waste. Please be my mother, wife, friend, treasure. I daily dream of us, be the mother of my children.

(With a cool voice and almost in a whisper) 'Sister Deborah, I love you...' (This were penetrating and melting words from bro Daniel).

'No'! Sister Deborah courageously spoke, 'I am not the one for you'.

(She paused and her voice changed, it suddenly became soft and soul alluring) 'Bro Daniel, I love you as a brother, not as a husband. I am not engaged and I would have loved to marry you, but after seeking Abba's face, He told me we are not meant for each other maritally but for the ministry. Your leading may be right but not on this'.

Bro Daniel interrupted.

'I am sure, God is not an author of confusion. He gave me several revelations and confirmations' (suddenly, sis Deborah perceived the oozing aroma of her burnt rice she was just trying to warm).

'What! This is burnt offering' (Bro Daniel was curious, he shouted, 'what is that?')

'My food got burnt while speaking with you' sister Deborah responded.

The nice brother said he would bring her food that night around 10:30 p.m.

Sister Deborah was about to respond when the Holy Spirit whispered in her spirit 'Deborah my daughter, don't collect that food, don't be ignorant of the vices of the enemy. That brother is not my marital son for you'. She jumped with a grateful heart.

Bro Daniel was trying to get out of his compound when she firmly said, 'Sir, kindly relieve yourself this stress, I will sort myself out (Immediately, she remembered Doris gave her a pack of chocolate biscuits and a can of malt).

That made her night.

The alarm started again and she managed to get to her reading table to have a conversation with God.

What do you think she was going to ask God?

With all sincerity, here was her prayer.

'Father, I love Daniel, he is my spec definition for a husband; he is rich, spiritual, tall, dark, handsome and even our purposes align. Father just a chance'.

Immediately, she heard it clearly from God

'DAUGHTER, HE IS NOT MY MARITAL WILL FOR YOU!

I know you had a long day and you have always wanted to know your husband, so tonight, I will reveal him to you, just be at alert to my spiritual beckoning, I will make it clear to you because you have been faithful to me all your life'.

With joy, she ran to her bed and was so connected. She was really anticipating who the lucky brother would be. God had never failed her, He could only delay her.

Deborah's face was lit with so much joy, she slept with a beautiful smile on her face.

Here comes the journey in her dream.

A brother came in from a corner of her church and they collided, the brother nearly fell her down, she couldn't catch her breath. The brother drew very close to her and the next words he whispered was....

Guess?

Who is this brother?

Could it be this brother?

Could God be this fair?

Is this dream valid?

Is this brother her spec?

CHAPTER TWO

Inspired by the Holy Spirit

A brother came in from a corner of her church and they collided, the brother nearly fell her down, she couldn't catch her breath, the brother drew very close to her and the next word he whispered was "You are the gift God gave me as my wife, will you marry me?"

Suddenly, sis Deborah's alarm started ringing and it interrupted her dream.

'Oh oh oh! You this alarm again, what is your mission? (Looking straight into her alarm clock and asking the rhetorical question), don't you know this is about my life, my husband to be, oh no, that is not my husband , chai, that can't be real, what am I even saying (she moved from the edge of her large, very comfortable bed)?

Can God be this unfair, why Bro Elijah? This dream must be a joke, this brother! This brother studied Mechanical engineering the last time I checked and here I am, a whole practicing Lawyer in a big firm.

(Continued soliloquizing as she moved with worries) "But God, our purpose do not align; he is very dark and I am very fair, he is too tall and I am the shorter version. Deborah (calling her name deeply with great tension) what will your children look like"?

(Suddenly, the voice of the Lord spoke loudly in the room)

STOP IT! HE IS MY SON FOR YOU!

(She turned around to see the speaker)

Whose voice is this? She asked.

'I AM THE LORD YOUR GOD'.

Immediately, she shuddered and knew she had no choice, Bro Elijah is the one for her maritally, that was her second deep encounter with God.

Wait a minute, have you ever had an encounter with God?

Do you know God?

Has he ever spoken to you? Why not make this a choice today. Know God for who He is, He is your Father.

(Back to story).

'Oh! Lord, I will accept your will' she reluctantly responded.

Immediately, her alarm rang again, it was time to prepare her food, then she remembered she had not done her quiet time.

Well, the day encounter was a enough for the day but she insisted on communicating with God.

Truthfully, the communication was very sweet and she enjoyed every bit of the koinonia until God reminded her of Bro Elijah, that was the end of her quiet time for the day.

Office was so stressful and she decided to gist her best friend about the recent update.

As she picked her phone to dial, the Holy Spirit came again. 'Don't tell anyone yet, it is for an appointed time'.

She disobeyed and called Becky her prayer partner and best friend.

Becky had always had an eye on Brother Elijah because he is the definition of TDH; he is tall, dark and handsome.

Who will not even like bro Elijah? The very conservative and reserved brother, so zealous of good work, a caring and cheerful giver, a deep baritone singer with an awesome voice, a spec for all sisters.

Immediately Becky heard this, her countenance changed, her mood changed, she suddenly became touchy and angry. It was very funny, a whole spiritual strong vibrant sister Becky cried, had stomach upset every second and the toilet became her home for the day. At least there is always water to wipe her tears away.

Fast forward to Beautiful Sunday Morning, sis Deborah is on her excessively long red gown with a touch of white flowers around the neck, she complimented the dress with a shining transparent pair of heels, coupled with a well tied scarf with a bow. Not only that, sis Deborah went to spa the previous day to exfoliate, so she was undauntedly radiant in all beauty and grace.

Who does not love a beautiful well dressed sister with brain?

Bro Daniel was the first to sight her as she carefully and graciously alighted from her car.

'Sister Debby Debby, you are looking exceptionally beautiful today. Wow, I can't wait to be your husband' (Bro Daniel whispered as he drew closed to her).

(Sis Deborah walked out of the scene quickly without a word).

Here is a new comer, a light skinned brother with well kept shining black beard. A glance of him would made you think he is from Europe, his skin is so clean that you barely can think of anything dirty, men and brethren, this guy is handsssssssoooooomeee! What! Just one person with all these

'Let all newcomers rise to their feet as we welcome them' The pastor said.

Fortunately the only new comer was this handsome brother.

Immediately sis Deborah sighted him from her seat, she smiled and whisper under her breath. 'Gosh! This guy his handsome, and I wish...'

'SHUT UP!' (the Holy Spirit spoke).

Immediately, she faced the preacher and she suddenly became troubled, then she knew there is a problem. Sis Deborah kept asking God 'Father, why this unrest?' but everything was silent.

After the sermon, the pastor said 'Sis Deborah, kindly wait after the service'.

Walking briskly to meet the pastor, she collided with Bro Elijah and the Holy Spirit came again this time directly 'This is your husband'..

With a deep frown, bro Elijah stood like a soldier and greeted 'Good afternoon, sis Deborah'.

She (Deborah), manages to answer but she was extremely pissed..

While greeting, the new handsome brother walked up to her with his best smile and his nice dimple and greeted.

'Hello Beautiful Sister, I am brother Donald and I am a lawyer, here is my card, you look so beautiful and your gown is so nice'.

With the best of smiles Sister Deborah also responded 'whaow, thanks so much, I am Deborah, just to think of it, I am also a lawyer, it is a pleasure meeting you, you can also have my card'.

(Everyone left into different direction to the same location)

As sister Deborah walked to meet the pastor, she saw Bro Elijah, Bro Daniel and the new handsome brother Donald staying close to each other discussing while waiting to see the pastor..

Everyone of them started smiling and trying to gain her attention except Bro Elijah.

On getting to the pastor's office, the first question pastor asked was 'Out of the three brothers, who are you led to?'

Immediately, she started having headache and suddenly became dumb.

Does it mean all these brothers are waiting to get married to her? Let me whisper it to you, YES they are waiting.

What do you think her response is now that she has met with a new spec that their purpose align?

Would she say Yes to bro Elijah that is frowning?

Or, is she going to say Yes to Daniel.

What do you think her response will be?

CHAPTER THREE

On getting to the Pastor's office, the first question the pastor asked was 'Out of the three brothers, who are you led to?'

Immediately, she started having headache and suddenly became dumb.

It became very hard for her to give a tangible reply, however, she struggled to say

'Pastor, I will pray about every one of them. I need to be clear, I will get back to you sir'.

She left with worries and a heavy heart because truthfully she has a deep crush on Brother Donald.

Lo and behold, sister Deborah could not sleep anymore. She became so restless, she just wanted to have a conversation with brother Donald...

Then she remembered she had his card, she grabbed it with great energy and boom! She is dialing uncle handsome's number.

I have a gist for you, did you know that brother Donald came to the fellowship because of Sister Deborah? He had seen her few days ago as she entered into the church and he sincerely loved her. He tried to do a very wonderful survey and he was assured he loved and wanted to settle with her.

Does it not sound so nice that sister Deborah's crush is intentionally ready to carry her to the altar?

Wow! The conversation started and here is our beautiful spiritual sister, rolling on the bed with the best of smile on her face, rolling her eye like she had just been given a lolly.

An hour of conversation and sis Deborah and Brother Donald had known deep into deep of each other.

Immediately The Holy Spirit came again with great warning

'Deborah, my daughter, be careful for the devil your adversary is around you, you are at the verge of falling into a big temptation'.

Spiritual sister Deborah ran into her study table and she started deep prayers to ensure she does not fall into this temptation.

As God would have His way, immediately she dropped the call, brother Elijah called and requested to have a date with her in one of the conservative restaurant.

'What!' She yelled!

Sister Deborah had no choice but to do her quiet time. While having the quiet time, the Holy Spirit ministered to her to ensure that she goes on the date and ignores Bro Donald call for the next few days.

It would have been possible to ignore the call but for the longing in her heart, and so at that moment, she began to feel that the warning was not from God, maybe it was just her conscience that was speaking to her.

She picked the call the next day and she got a very strong warning from God but she was beginning to allow her self to dominate and this was refraining the Holy Spirit from her.

It's Wednesday already, the suppose day for her to visit Bro Elijah but here is sister Deborah very reluctant to move to the restaurant. Well, according to divine instruction, she did.

Have you ever seen handsome brother Elijah before, that Wednesday was a different one, he is on his amazing polo shirt with a jean trouser and a very nice footwear. His hair was properly kept and he looks cooler and dashing that awesome afternoon.

Well, why won't he? My dear, it is a proposal something.

Sis Deborah was wowed at his appearance. She couldn't deny the fact that he

CHAPTER FOUR

Inspired by Holy Spirit

'The car is yours and I love you so much, I can't keep this anymore in me, I would have waited for more time to say this but you are worth more than gold to me. I know this is coming so soon. Darling, I can't deny loving you and I can't love you less. Will you marry me?'

Sis Deborah went blank, she was overwhelmed with mixed joy, she wanted a new car, however, she was contemplating accepting the gift. Besides, she loved Donald so much.

While still silent, Donald moved close and drew her hand close, immediately there was a charge in her body like a sweet electrifying shock. No! Donald don't touch me.

She responded 'Donald, I will give you a response later, let me have a conversation with my pastor'.

As Donald moved backwards, he whispered 'I deeply love you and I will always love, this is coming from a genuine heart'.

Immediately, she collected the key and left to her apartment.

Running to her bed to talk to God, she started crying, letting out her whole emotions to God.

Truthfully, Bro Elijah was the one God has for her but, he was not caring, was always frowning and anytime she tried to speak to him or make any friendly moves, he changed the subject and made it seem she was forcing herself on him. As it is well known, no lady loves to be seen as been pushy, however, when a woman loves a man, she can do anything for the man, she can go extra mile for him and would reject every other brother that comes her way.

Here comes Sister Deborah insecurity as she thinks aloud 'what if he is just led but he does not love me? He never said he loved me for once.

Okay, it is fine if he does not say he loves me, but at least, he should say he loves my personality, my dreams, vibes, actions. If I am not his spec and I am not his type and he is led, would he accept me? Would he treat me well? Won't he go for someone he truly loves later and leaves me high and dry? God, you cannot leave me like this, what should I do?'

(Changing position with worries in her voice, she cried to heaven).

'Dear Lord, I love Donald and he loves me too, I care for him and everything around him shows that he loves me, just give me the chance to be his wife, I am not sure I can cope with Bro Elijah. He is just too uptight and he is less romantic, he makes me feel less of myself'.

A whisper from God dropped into her heart 'Dear daughter, I know the desire of thy heart, but my will for you is ELIJAH'.

But God....

A message came into her phone and interrupted her. As she checked the message, it is from Sister Becky

' Hello Pretty, how are you? I hope you are doing great. While I was praying this morning, the Spirit of God spoke to me and I sensed in my spirit to tell you this.

Isaiah 40:5

'And the glory of the Lord shall be revealed, and all flesh shall see it together, for the mouth of Lord has spoken it'.

Anything God says you should do, Debbie Love, just do it for it is from God'.

Oh! Oh! Oh! God! I don't want Bro Elijah, he makes me feel less of myself, he does not value me, he is too spiritual that he forgets to be romantic. We can't cope.

Lord! I know you have spoken but on this please let me go with Donald.

Afterall, there are people who are not your children and they have good homes.

Lord on this, let me choose. I want Donald.

She left for her bed.

Scrolling through her phone to message a client, she saw Brother Donald's message.

'Sister Debby, as I was praying this night, the Lord told me you have accepted my proposal. Darling, I still love you, please don't play hard on me. I can't wait to take you to the altar.

Also, can we go on a date tomorrow at Three Stars hotel...

She smiled beautifully and her mind became so fixed to say her Yes to Donald.

It was a wonderful day with Donald, he bathed her with sweet words and lavished her with gifts and goodies.

Here is Sunday and Sis Deborah is super excited she would be seeing the love of her life.

She got to the church and all her mind was on Donald.

Finally, she got to pastor's office and explained everything to him. She was ready to go with Donald.

The pastor was not convinced and he felt so troubled. He asked salient questions and she was smart with the response as a lawyer.

Lo and behold, sister Deborah was going to say Yes to bro Donald and NO to brother Elijah..

What did you think will happen on this day?

How will Bro Elijah feel?

How will Donald feel?

What did you think should be corrected?

What word do you have for bro Elijah and Sister Deborah?

Do you think God will still intervene?

Do you think God will allow her to say Yes to bro
Donald?

CHAPTER FIVE

Walking with confidence to give her replies to each and everyone.

The Holy Spirit came the last time and said, ' Elijah, is my son for you'.

She shunned the voice and spoke to herself

'Donald is mine. I have never experienced love in this dimension before. He tells me how he constantly loves me, he shows it with everything he have unlike Bro Elijah that only told me he loves me twice, he hardly calls, he hardly talks to me. How am I sure that he really loves me?'

While still moving towards the back of the church, she saw Bro Elijah and she was very peaceful and assured he was the one. This time bro Elijah was not smiling neither did he look like someone who was ready for any conversation.

He was praying in his Spirit as the Holy Spirit already revealed the manipulations in his marital life.

No sooner had they bumped into each other than bro Elijah grabbed Sis Deborah's hand trying to tell her something but he was too harsh. He wasn't soft on her and the devil that wanted sister Deborah to miss it maritally started operation.

Sis Deborah looked straight into Bro Elijah eye and said, ' No! We cannot marry!'

Bro Elijah eyes became heavy and in seconds, tears started dripping like rain.

As an emotional being, Sister Deborah could not stand the emotions, she left him unattended to.

On her way to the gate, she saw Mr loving and handsome Donald. Donald had sensed that she would say YES to him. So, he had made preparation for a grand proposal with his friends.

'Debby love, how are you? You are spinning grace and beauty today? You look ravishingly breathtaking. I would like us to go out today. Please don't say NO!'

She sheepishly followed while blushing in her heart and at that moment, sis Doris called

'Hello Pretty! How are you? Where are you? I want you to help lead a prayer by 4:00p.m. today. Some sisters will be in my place. Please darling, don't say No. Deborah I also feel prompted in my spirit to warn you of the devices of the enemy, my darling be careful'.

'Okay, thanks, I have heard you, I am in the middle of something, I will try to come by 4:00p.m. You know this is impromptu though, but for the sake of kingdom friendship, I got you covered. See you later, I love you'

She hung the call.

As she got into the suite, she was overwhelmed by what she saw.

Thanks to Donald's friends, they did a great word, the decoration was massive!

Everywhere is painted white and red. This proposal is grand style.

While in the awesomeness of the moment coupled with a solemn song of Celine Dion, Donald went on his knee with the question,

'Sister Debby you are the best thing that ever happened to me. Words will fail me right now to describe how ardently I love you. Please will you marry me?'.

With overwhelming excitement in her voice, she screamed YES!

Her phone rang, it was Becky. It was then she remembered she had a prayer to hold.

She excused herself and left for the prayer.

Becky was ministering when she got there.

Every single word she was saying was pointing to Deborah. Becky spoke extensively on choosing

God over self; allowing God take over situation and not choosing by sight.

Every word penetrated Sis Deborah, with no time tears started flowing down her eyes and she knew she had gotten it wrong.

She led the prayer and God was glorified..

The words kept ringing in her subconscious mind, she kept crying to God.

Do you think she will say Yes to Bro Elijah now that she has realized her mistake?

Do you think Bro Elijah will accept her back?

Do you think, she would reverse the YES she told Bro Donald?

If yes, how will Donald feel?

Who do you think Donald is?

CHAPTER SIX

Getting to the house after a long time with God at Becky's place, Donald called to thank her.

Then he began his love story again and made countless promises, all the promises are like a newly refined gold.

Truthfully, Donald loves Sister Deborah so much. It is beyond mere infatuation, he is really in love with her, but there are some lapses..

She couldn't hold her emotions again, she began to also start saying many sweet nonsense, her emotion banks were full and she was overwhelmingly in love with Donald.

Sister Deborah told her pastor and parents about her finally taken decision to marry Donald.

Every preparation on health and some other background check were done.

It was time for introduction and parental consent.

Would her parents be discerning enough to know their daughter is doing the wrong thing?

Well, Donald dressed in a very responsible way. He was looking so great.

The physical appearance was acceptable to Deborah's parents but her spiritual mother was not convinced. God at one time revealed a dark brother in person of Elijah to her, so she was surprised her daughter wanted to marry someone contrary to what she saw.

Gbam! Deborah's mummy cannot contain the emotion. She quietly called her daughter into her room, asked her of her conviction, her belief, her assurance and Deborah convincingly said she wanted to marry Donald.

What can a concerned mother do? She is not going to force anything on her daughter.

The parental consent from Deborah side was over and it was Donald family.

Who doesn't want their child to marry a lawyer? Who don't want a pretty lady in the family?

Donald's parents were so glad to accept Deborah, most especially because of her beauty and influence but they were shocked that their son Donald wanted to get married to a committed sister of God.

It was shocking!

Did they have a choice? Since that is their son's choice and she is pretty enough with influence, they decided to dance to his tune.

It was wedding time and Deborah's parents were not fully happy their daughter is getting married to Donald.

What is it about Donald?

Donald is not a committed child of God, truth be told, he is just a church goer and he doesn't even have that deep love for God.

He became committed to service because of Deborah.

Now he has what he wants.

The wedding was beyond ceremonial, it was grand and massive. Billions were spent on the wedding, this is one interesting wedding a Christian would do.

Since Donald is not a true christian, what will happen next?

Guess what the home will look like?

Would Deborah realize early and what would be her next action?

Can she save him?

Will this marriage work? After all there are many who have not known the Lord but their marriages are sweet.

CHAPTER SEVEN

At this time, the spirit of God had departed and she was carried away by the niceness and all.

They travelled out for their honeymoon as this was part of their plan.

It was night and it was time for couple's game, this was where the beast in Donald arose.

Prior to this time, Donald has always been a womanizer and he is a sadistic dacryphiles (someone that derives pleasure in seeing tears during sex). He practically gets prostitutes and pays for this act because he finds pleasure in it.

Truth be told, he really loves Deborah and that was why he went for her but he is addicted to this sexual lifestyle.

So, he had no choice but to treat her that way, and being new to the system, she thought every pain she experienced was because she was just breaking her hymen.

But at another point it was severe and he started beating her despite the excruciating pain just to see her cry.

Sis Deborah was welcomed into this lifestyle for days until reality dawned on her about Donald's personality.

Donald is a very nice person except for the fact that he has addictions and he is a drunkard and so in order to make up for his misbehaviour, he begged her daily and did many other things to pamper her.

It got to a time Deborah could not endure it and she became reluctant in bed, so Donald started bringing prostitutes into the house and some of his friends that are birds of the same feathers would forcefully sleep with Deborah.

Her life became terrible day by day and there was really no one to rescue her, besides she felt the guilt anytime she wants to call on God.

Then, she tried to speak with one of Donald's friend, Bright.

Bright understood her plight because he knew who she was and he knew his friend.

Here a plan was drafted.

Bright promised to take her back home, give her accommodation and make life better for her on Donald's birthday which was in two weeks time. Bright knew Donald will be drunk and unconscious so the plan would work out well.

Unfortunately, Donald was at the stair case of the duplex eavesdropping on their conversation.

He pretended like he knew nothing and went back upstairs to plan.

Then he started his plan with his friends. Deborah had always looked for every means to escape but it never worked out because Donald had always been the antagonist.

Now, he knows the new plan, how will Deborah escape?

Would God make a way?

She is broken, will she be bruised after.

Who will rescue her?

CHAPTER EIGHT

Prior to Donald's birthday, he made plans with his ungodly friends that they would make Bright drunk.

The plan was successfully orchestrated and Deborah was not left out in the nefarious game. Her drink was drugged and she was also drunk.

They made Bright sleep with Deborah unconsciously. Bright wouldn't know because he was drunk and he was used to sleeping with prostitutes, so, he thought it was one of them, since it is Donald's birthday.

He woke up the next morning to see Deborah beside him and he became disappointed, she was still unconscious.

Then Bright remembered his promise and plan, he felt so pained and bitter but he determined not to give up.

Donald and his friends were drunk and asleep and Bright knew that was his cue to execute his plan.

He managed to get Deborah off the bed and tried to find her already packed bags.

Then the door creaked and he became scared that Donald was awake.

Fortunately, it was the maid, so he tactically took the bags out and managed to wake Deborah from her deep sleep. She became alert and smart immediately she remembered the plan.

Narrowly, they escaped from the house. No sooner had they left the house than Donald woke and suspecting that they had left, immediately drove to the airport.

Fortunately, God being the ever faithful One He is, ensured that the moment they left the airport to Nigeria was when Donald arrived at the airport.

He did a thorough search, then reality dawned on him that his wife was no longer with him, she has left.

As he was going back home baffled, he had a fatal accident and he died instantly.

Deborah's phone started ringing but she was still aching from the trauma, so she was not in the best mood to pick any calls.

As Bright turned his phone on, he was surprised as he saw the post of Donald's death but he was not sure if he should tell Deborah because of her state.

Unfortunately, Deborah was shocked when she also saw the news while trying to check something online.

She wept but she was quite happy. It was a mixed feeling.

Congratulations! She was back in Nigeria and she felt peace like a billow roll.

Bright got an hotel for her and she lodged there for days until a day when she decided to stroll early in the morning, that she heard the word of God. Every single word from the preacher touched her, she remembered who she used to be, she remembered her intimacy with God, she broke down in tears and all she could do was to run back home and tried to start over with God.

Guess who she saw? Guess the preacher? It is Bro Elijah. No! She is not sure, yes, she is sure.

"Sis Deborah!", "Bro Elijah!", they both called their names simultaneously.

They had a wonderful conversation, then Bro Elijah asked about her husband and with mixed feelings Deborah explained everything..

It is unfortunately fortunate that Bro Elijah will be getting married to Sis Becky in few weeks time.

Bro Elijah had an intense conversation on God's light and mercy and she found her way back to God.

She came back home revived and she knew she needed more of God, then the spiritual lion in her began to roar and she was thirsty for God.

It is Sunday and Deborah and Bright went for service, it was a wonderful service and one of the kind.

Every words from the pulpit melted Bright. Bright's parents are pastors and his mother spoke to him the night before the service to come to Christ and so coupled with the Sunday message, he prayed earnestly and gave his life to Christ.

He became transformed and a committed son for God.

Sis Deborah managed to reach her parents, she was welcomed home and was lucky to be accepted back in her place of work, she started life again and became more committed to God.

It was at sister Becky and Brother Elijah's wedding, she cried and all she could say remains 'It is good to do the will of God'.

The last time I checked sis Deborah in this fictional story, she is still single and committed to God.

THE END